Pippin and Pudding

For Smokey, Lucky, Toby, Pippin, Freddy, Pixie, Thomas, Marigold, Widdershins and Grig — K.V.J.

For Roberta and her dog, Fletcher, with many thanks ... you're the coolest! — B.L.

Text © 2001 K.V. Johansen
Illustrations © 2001 Bernice Lum

Kids Can Press acknowledges the financial support of the Ontario Arts Council, the Canada Council for the Arts and the Government of Canada, through the BPIDP, for our publishing activity.

Published in Canada by
Kids Can Press Ltd.
29 Birch Avenue
Toronto, ON M4V 1E2

Published in the U.S. by
Kids Can Press Ltd.
2250 Military Road
Tonawanda, NY 14150

www.kidscanpress.com

The artwork in this book was rendered in watercolor and marker.
The text is set in Smile.

Edited by Debbie Rogosin
Designed by Marie Bartholomew
Printed and bound in Hong Kong, China, by Book Art Inc., Toronto

The hardcover edition of this book is smyth sewn casebound.
The paperback edition of this book is limp sewn with a drawn-on cover.

CM 01 0 9 8 7 6 5 4 3 2 1
CM PA 02 0 9 8 7 6 5 4 3 2 1

National Library of Canada Cataloguing in Publication Data

Johansen, K. V. (Krista V.), 1968–
Pippin and Pudding

(Pippin and Mabel)
ISBN 1-55074-631-6 (bound).   ISBN 1-55337-418-5 (pbk.)

I. Lum, Bernice II. Title. III. Series: Johansen, K. V. (Krista V.), 1968– . Pippin and Mabel.

PS8569.02676P553 2001   jC813`.54   C00-931639-6
PZ7.J64Pi 2001

Kids Can Press is a [*Corus*™] Entertainment company

Pippin and Pudding

Story by K.V. Johansen

Illustrations by Bernice Lum

Kids Can Press

Pippin was a yellow dog with great big ears and a curly black tail. She loved Mabel, and Mabel loved her, and they were happy together in their little house near the woods.

One day when Mabel was busy, Pippin went to the woods by herself. She was sniffing a bush — sniff, snuff, snuffle — when she heard a sound. "Mew!"

Pippin stuck her nose in under the leaves. "Fsssst!"

She jumped back and lay down where she could watch the bush. Pippin watched it for a very long time. Then she heard a "Prrr-rrr-rrr," and a fluffy gray kitten crept out.

The kitten rubbed against Pippin.

"Prrr-rrr-rrr," he said.

Pippin wagged her tail and rolled the kitten over with her paw. The kitten dashed away. Pippin raced after him. Sproing! The kitten sprang out from behind a tree and chased Pippin through the ferns.

Pippin and the kitten played in the woods all morning. When Pippin went home, the kitten followed her.

"Oh my," said Mabel, and she picked up the kitten. "Where did you come from?"

"Prrr-rrr-rrr," said the kitten.

"He must have gotten lost," said Mabel. "We'd better try to find his owner." That afternoon she made a sign and put it up in the post office, where everyone would see it.

Pippin and the kitten had fun playing together. First the kitten hid behind a door and pounced on Pippin. Then Pippin chased the kitten around the living room. The kitten chased Pippin up and down the stairs.

Whoosh! They slid across the hall. Bang! went a table. Crash! went a vase.

"Out! Out! Out!" said Mabel, and she chased them both outside.

At bedtime, Pippin went to
sleep on her blanket, and the

kitten went to sleep on a pillow. When Pippin woke

up in the morning, the kitten was curled

up beside her. She licked his

ears. He batted her nose,
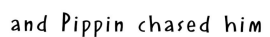
and Pippin chased him

upstairs. Thump! Oof! They

bounced onto Mabel's bed.

"Out! Out! Out!" cried

Mabel, and she chased

them both outside.

For two days, Pippin and
the kitten ate together, slept
together and played together,

but on the third day, the telephone rang.

The kitten's owner was coming to

take him home.

Pippin was sad. Her ears drooped

and her tail drooped. When Mabel

wasn't looking, Pippin crept upstairs.

"Woof," she said, very quietly.

"Mew?" said the kitten,

and he followed Pippin.

Pippin climbed the steep narrow stairs to the attic. It was full of spiders and cobwebs and old boxes. There were lots of places to hide. Pippin picked the kitten up by the scruff of the neck and carefully put him in a big box.

"Mew!" said the kitten.

Pippin got her favorite bone and put it in the box with the kitten, so he'd have something to chew on. Then she went downstairs.

Soon there was a knock at the door.

"Hello," said the man. "I've come about my kitten."

Mabel and the man went to the kitchen. "Kitty, kitty, kitty," they called. There was no kitten in the kitchen. They looked in the dining room. "Here, kitty, kitty, kitty!" But there was no kitten in the dining room either. They looked in the living room.

"Pippin," said Mabel, "have you seen the kitten?"

"Woof," said Pippin.

Mabel looked more closely at Pippin. "Why are you covered in cobwebs?" she asked. And then she said, "Aha!"

Mabel and the man went up to
the attic. Pippin followed them.
Mabel started to look in the boxes,
and she found the bone. "Oh Pippin," she said.
Mabel took the kitten out and gave him
to the man.

"Thank you," he said. "Say, your dog seems to like this kitten. Would you like to keep him? I have three more at home."

"Hmm," said Mabel. "No thank you. Pippin and I are quite happy here on our own."

So the man took the kitten home.

Pippin moped. There was no one to chase around the house. There was no one to cuddle with at night. There was no one to play with while Mabel was busy. Pippin was so sad that she wouldn't even eat her supper. She moped for a whole week.

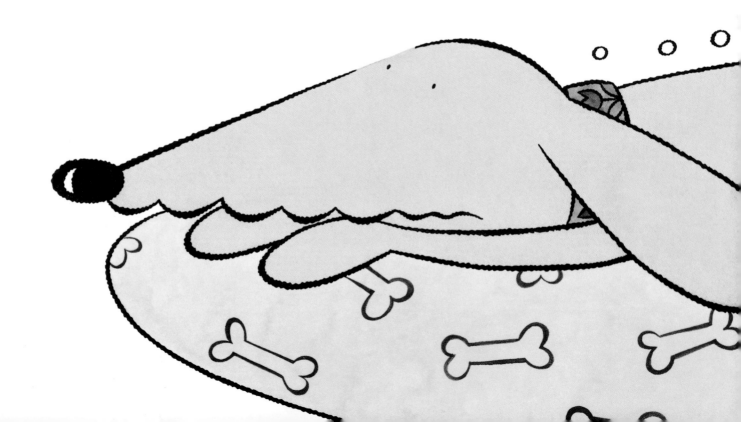

"Oh dear," said Mabel. You really miss that kitten, don't you, Pippin?"

Mabel got her car keys. "I'll be back soon," she said, and she drove away.

Pippin flopped down on her blanket and took a nap. She heard Mabel come home, but she didn't get up. Then she heard a "Prrr-rrr-rrr."

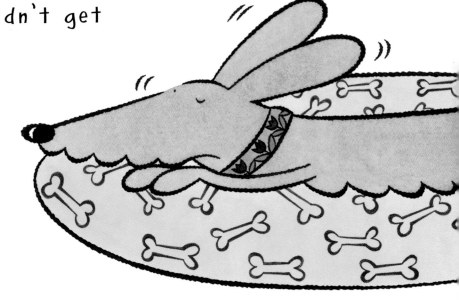

Pippin opened her eyes.

"Woof!" she said, and she

bounced up and down and wagged her tail.

"Prrr-rrr-rrr," said the kitten.

"I think Pudding would be a good name for such

a round fluffy kitten," said Mabel. "What do you

think, Pippin?"

"Woof!" said Pippin.

Pudding jumped out of Mabel's

arms and chased Pippin around

the house.

Pippin chased Pudding up and down the
stairs. Mew! Woof! Bang! Crash!

"Out! Out! Out!" laughed
Mabel, and she chased them
both outside.

Then Mabel put on her boots and went outside, too, and they all went for a walk together.

In the woods, Pudding found something. He poked it with his paw. Hop! Pippin snuffled it all over with her nose. Hop!

Poke! Hop! Snuffle! Hop! They made that toad hop all the way over to Mabel.

"Mew!" said Pudding.

"Woof!" said Pippin.

The toad looked at Mabel. Mabel looked at the toad.

"Absolutely not!" said Mabel. "Two animals are quite enough in one little house. Now come along. It's time to go home."

When they got home, Mabel opened
the door and ...

Hop! went the toad.

"Oh dear," said Mabel.